This is Not A Classroom

Gladys Adeleye

ISBN:1537044281
ISBN-13: 978-1537044286

DEDICATION

To my students;
Past and present.

CONTENTS

ACKNOWLEDGMENTS

My gratitude goes to my Lord and Saviour, Jesus Christ for life and inspiration. To my family and friends for time, effort and financial support.
Then to my mother, Alice Aguele; for her incessant prayers.

Chapter 1

"I Like KFC"

I absolutely hated school and all that came with it – until I met Mrs. A. H. Don't ask me what A. H. stands for because as hard as we tried, she refused to tell us. Each time we tried to persist, she gave us an evil look that sent shivers down our spines. Then, when we found out the head teacher was dead scared of her, we gave up trying. (And that's true: Mr. Oakley, the head teacher, was very scared of Mrs. A. H. Everyone was scared of Mrs. A H!)

I still remember the first day she came into our classroom. It was a typical Friday morning. The bell had rang, and since our teacher was yet to arrive, every student was doing his or her own thing.

Suddenly, the door flung open. "Hello!" came from this massive voice. It wasn't a man's voice, but it sounded so strong that we all turned in unison to see this ginormous[1] woman waddle into our classroom.

Usually, we would've burst into laughter, but as if we'd all been hypnotized, we said, "Hello," in return.

As she settled her big bag of books on the desk, she said, "My name is Mrs. A. H., and I like KFC chicken."

The whole class burst into laughter!

Then she put her hand up and asked, "Can you all be quiet, please?"

But no one paid her any attention. So after asking a couple of times without a response, she banged her hand on the desk and shouted, "Shuuuuttt up!"

---

[1] Ginormous is a word made up by combining gigantic and enormous and is used by children to describe something or someone really big.

Bingo, the class fell silent.

"Good," she said with a nod and a smile. Then she called the names on the register.

That done, she wrote "Balanced Diet" on the whiteboard and turned round to face the class.

"Well, today's topic is a fascinating and important one because, as young people, you need to be taught the right reasons for eating a balanced diet. If you don't, you'll just end up looking like me."

We all wanted to burst into laughter again, but we didn't. We were afraid of this new, crazy teacher, and a few of us just wanted to show some respect.

Then she turned to the left side of the room and pointed at Sam. "Boy, what's your name?"

"Bob," he replied. Everyone laughed because we knew the truth.

"Really? I would have thought you looked more like an Adolf."

"Adolf!" everyone shouted, laughing at the top of their lungs. Sam was so surprised that he put his hand up.

Mrs. A. H. said to him, "Put your hand down, Adolf. I need to carry on with the lesson."

"But my name is Sam, not Adolf."

"Oh, yes it is. And as long as I'm in this school, Adolf shall be your name, kid."

"But you can't do that. My name is Sam."

"Well, I will, and next time you'll know not to mock about when I ask you questions. OK?"

Then to the rest of the class, she asked, "Now, where were we?"

Sam interrupted. "But I'm not going to let you carry on until you call me by my real name."

"Really? You actually want to stop me from doing my job? Huh." She giggled. "I wouldn't do that if I were you."

"Well, I wouldn't eat so much KFC if I were you."

"No? Why not?"

"Obviously," Sam said sarcastically, "so you can fit through the door for starters!"

The whole class gasped. "Uuuuhhhh!"

"I warn you, kid, in your own best interest, turn back from this path. It only leads to destruction. I'm warning you."

"And what will you do if I don't?"

At that question, Mrs. A. H. went over to Sam, picked him up as if he were merely a feather, and threw him through the window.

As if that wasn't shocking enough, she threw him the brush and dustpan and said, "And do sweep up the broken glass."

To say we were stunned is an understatement.

"Well, who's next? Or shall I carry on with my lesson in peace?"

We were all so dumbstruck that everyone just nodded.

"Good. Now, let's pick up from where we left it."

At that moment the bell rang. We dashed out of the classroom, leaving our bags behind.

Chapter 2

Moon-walking Hairline

The following morning, Sam came to school with his right hand hanging off a sling. His dad followed, and he was as mad as a hornet. Everyone was eager to see how Sam's father's meeting with Mrs. A. H. would turn out. Sadly, though, we were certain all of us would miss the show until, of course, juicy rumors began flying around school. The pain of having to wait that long to lay hold of such a piping-hot rumor as this; was pure torture!

These and many more were the thoughts plaguing my heart as I walked sluggishly towards my French lesson. Thus, deeply lost in thought, I failed to notice when Alfred (my clumsy, mindless classmate); walked into the classroom without holding the door behind him. Naturally, the door swung right into my face, and *bang!* I lost consciousness. The next time I opened my eyes, I was lying on one of the beds in the sickbay. My head hurt terribly.

"Thank God you're awake." It was the voice of Linda, the school first-aider. "I was so worried about you that I called the paramedics. One of them should be here any minute now. So how do you feel?" she asked, gently patting my shoulder.

"My head hurts. Ouch!" I replied as I attempted to sit up.

"I can imagine how much it hurts. That door is very strong, and walking into it the way you did ... what on earth were you thinking about?"

I wasn't sure if this was a rhetorical question, but trust me, she wouldn't want to know the answer. So I just let out another cry of pain.

Before she could say another word, the paramedic walked into the room, led by a student envoy. He walked over to my bedside as Linda began to explain some kind of gibberish[2] to him. Well, I say gibberish because as soon as Linda began to speak, I suddenly realized the room I was lying in was next to meeting room 2. This was where the all-important meeting between Mr

---

[2] Gibberish is unintelligible or meaningless speech or writing; nonsense.

Barthurst, Sam's father, and Mrs. A. H. was to take place that morning.

What! I thought. *Does this mean I can actually get the gist*[3] *firsthand, like, live? Wow, I'm going to do whatever it takes to keep me in this bed and in this room until that meeting is over. Yippee!*

Luckily, I didn't have to do much to achieve that because after examining me, the paramedic instructed Linda to ensure I lay in bed for a couple of hours and to give me another dose of paracetamol[4]. I couldn't believe my ears.

The accident was actually turning out to be a blessing in disguise. Just as Madame La' Ponte, my French teacher, would say, *"Tout est bien qui finit bien!"* ("All's well that ends well!") I'm not even sure that's proper French, but there you go; you know who to blame for my bad French.

As the paramedic got ready to leave, he repeated his

---

[3] Gist is the general detail of something, like a meeting.

[4] Paracetamol –a medicine like Tylenol.

instructions to Linda, adding that I didn't need to be taken to hospital because the cold pad had already done my head a lot of good. Then he walked out of the room with Linda following.

Wow, this is better than magic, I thought. *I'll get to hear every bit of the conversation between—*

But before I could complete that thought, I heard a furious voice ask, "So where is the teacher who threw my son out the window? Where is she?" It was Sam's father.

Then I heard the head teacher reply, "Please, calm down, Mr Barthurst; calm down. We can settle this amicably, you know. Please take a seat. I beg you. Please."

"No, Mr Head Teacher, I will not take a seat, and I will not calm down until I see this Mrs. A. H. or whatever she calls herself."

"Oh my, this is really getting hot," I whispered to myself, sitting up on the bed. "I wonder if there's a way I can actually see this show live!"

Looking around, I noticed a door linking this room with the meeting room. Wondering if it would work, I tiptoed towards it and looked through the keyhole. *Voila!* I could clearly see everything.

At that moment Mrs. A. H. appeared and announced, "Well, here I am!"

Her sudden entrance startled the two men. I could tell the head teacher was anxious because his forehead suddenly wrinkled with a deep sense of anxiety.

Mrs. A. H. asked, "Well, Mr Oakley was anybody asking to see me or what?"

The head teacher finally recovered and walked towards Mrs. A. H. But as he began to say something, Mr Barthurst interrupted with, "Yes, I'm the one demanding to see you. I'm Sam's father." He had obviously recovered too.

"Well, I am she. How may I help?"

"What do you mean, how may you help? How dare you do

this to my son! How dare you!" He charged towards her as he shouted.

The head teacher feared the worst, so he quickly made his way to block Mr Barthurst from moving any closer to Mrs. A. H.

"He got what he deserved for calling me fat."

"Well, he was obviously stating the fact, wasn't he?"

"Oh my God; can we please resolve this amicably?" Mr. Oakley asked, trying to squelch the amassing inferno.

"Well, Mr. whatever-you-call-yourself, let me state some facts to you here: Fact number one – if you would've eaten a sufficient amount of peas growing up, you'd have at least been three inches taller than a midget. And if you'd paid any attention to your broccoli, it would have taken a couple more years before your hairline started moon-walking. F-A-C-T number two!" Mrs. A. H., towering over Mr Barthurst, shouted.

The head teacher attempted once more to calm the situation, but as he wasn't particularly tall either, his efforts didn't yield much result. In frustration, he sank into his chair.

"Wha-wha-what? Mr. Barthurst stammered. "This isn't happening." Turning to face the head teacher, he said, "Mr. Oakley, don't make me believe you're incapable of controlling your teachers. How dare she speak to me in this manner? I demand that this teacher be sacked immediately."

"Yeah, go on, blame me. Be mad at me; just like the days of Socrates and Plato,[5] blame the teacher for everything. But on the flipside, every parent is innocent; every parent has every right to speak to teachers the way you talked to me."

"Mr. Oakley act now and sack her!" Mr. Barthurst shouted.

"What exactly do you know about hiring and firing of teachers? Yes, tell me, what do you know?" Mrs. A. H. said, not

---

[5] Socrates was the first teacher in ancient Greece to be blamed for corrupting the youths of Athens with his philosophies; Plato was his student.

moving from where she stood.

"You deserve the sack!"

"Says who and why?" Mrs. A. H. asked. But before anyone could respond, she walked over to Mr Oakley's table and said, "Dear Mr. Oakley, if you weren't such a doodle head, you would've issued this parent a bill for the smashed glass. Yes, he should pay for it."

"What? A bill for the smashed glass? This must be a joke! You dare talk about a flipping glass after you gave my son a broken arm?"

"Well, before that kid came into my lesson, you gave him a broken life!"

"Huh?" He gasped.

"Yes indeed – bad parents make bad children."

"Somebody please wake me from this terrible nightmare. This isn't true. Am I still on planet Earth or what?"

"No, darling. Welcome to planet Stupid!"

This made Mr Bathurst's jaw drop in utter amazement.

As he stood, stunned, not saying a word, Mrs. A. H. turned swiftly and said to him, "I thought so too. End of discussion."

Throwing her hand up in the air, she said, "Bye, y'all," and marched towards the door. As she pulled the door handle, she turned round to look at the two men gazing at her in utter amazement.

She smirked and whispered, *"lol,"*[6] and stepped out of the room.

As I turned round to return to my bed, Linda stood at the door with hands folded across her chest. I wished – sorry, I mean prayed – for the ground to open up and swallow me. I stood there dumbfounded.

She said, "So you were only pretending to be in pain, right? Why?"

"I was er, er, er …" I tried to mumble some words but none formed.

Looking sternly at me, she said, "To teach you never to do such again, you will serve a two-day lunch detention in my office. That'll enable you catch up on what you missed in your French lesson today."

"Phew!" I sighed in relief. *Two days of lunch detention is a small price to pay for this story I'm about to go spread round the*

---

[6] LOL: laugh out loud.

whole school! I thought.

"And what are you still standing there thinking about? Get going. It's nearly time for the second lesson, you know. Come on, run along," she urged me, and I ran out of the sickbay towards my classroom.

Chapter 3

On the Bus

By the end of school that day, news had gone round that I had details of the meeting, so when I came out of my classroom, at least twenty students were waiting to hear it from me. Being the business-minded person I'd always been, I used the opportunity to make a few pounds. I announced that whoever wanted to hear the details must pay me fifty pence. Without any form of resistance, eight of the twenty students handed me their 50p coin. Keeping the money safe in my bag, I told the other students to go away.

Those who had paid joined in, and within a few minutes, it was just the eight students and me walking towards the bus stop. I then gave them a download of the meeting between Mr Bathurst and Mrs. A. H. that morning, adding a few flavours of mine wherever possible. Everyone laughed so loudly as I relayed the story that we didn't realize that a member of staff had been walking quietly behind us. As we saw the bus approaching, we all began to run towards the bus. It was as we got onto the bus that we realized which teacher had been walking behind us. It was Mrs. A. H.!

Two questions were on everybody's mind as Mrs. A. H. paid her bus fare and walked to take a seat in one of the seats at the right-hand side of the bus: Why was Mrs. A. H. on the public bus, and how much of our conversation about her meeting this morning did she hear? We knew she had a car and had never taken the public bus before, at least not with the students. If she had, news would have got around. My curiosity got the better of me, and I decided to have a little conversation with her. If I could muster the courage, I would ask why she was taking the public bus.

However, as I made to get out of my chair, I saw Mrs. A. H. starting a not-so-friendly conversation with one of the boys sitting in front of her.

"Could you turn the volume of your music down, please?" asked Mrs. A. H., trying very hard to be polite, but the boy refused to listen or do as he was told.

Mrs. A. H. said in a much louder tone, "You need to turn it

down. You've got earphones on, so I'm not supposed to hear it. Turn the volume down."

Taking off one of his earphones, the boy replied, "Well, if you don't want to hear it, why don't you shut your ears!"

"Well, you shut your mouth and turn it down!"

In anger, the boy turned up the volume much louder. We wondered what she would do next.

Mrs. A. H. moved out of her seat and sat directly behind this boy. Then she got the exact same type of phone out of her bag and selected some really annoying African song that sounded as if the singer had just woken up from a thirty-day sleep. She put the volume of this song so high and placed it behind the boy's ear.

It was so hilarious that we all burst out laughing, but the kid didn't find this funny at all, so he pushed the stop button and got off at the very next stop, his music completely turned off.

As he got off the bus, Mrs. A. H. called out to him, "It's gonna be at least half an hour before the next bus arrives, so enjoy the cold weather, ha-ha-ha!" This made some people laugh even more.

As we came to a bend, Mrs. A. H. left her seat and walked towards the driver. When he pulled up at the next stop, we heard her ask if he went past a particular garage. That was how we guessed her car was parked in a garage or something. We had a football practice, so we didn't leave School at the usual time. As a result, there were more students from the neighbouring school on that particular bus.

As Mrs. A. H. stood there listening to the driver's explanation of how to get to the garage, a banana peel flew all the way across the bus and hit her in the back of her head.

We all gasped in shock while the other students from the neighbouring school found it funny.

Then, in slow motion, Mrs. A. H. turned around, gently put her pen and notepad into her bag, picked up the banana peel, and walked towards us. I so wanted to explain that I was not involved in any way, shape, or form, but those other students were in hysterics. Mrs. A. H. figured out that it must have been one of them who threw the peel.

Still holding the banana peel, she slowly approached the group of boys. She shouted, "Who done it?"

Crippled with fear, the kids pointed in unison towards the culprit. Perhaps if he had stopped laughing or denied it, Mrs. A. H. would have let it go.

But this boy stood up and threw his hands in the air, saying, "Yeah, I done it. *Who're you gonna do 'bout 'e, whor-guan-man?"*[7], trying to mimic the Jamaican accent.[8]

Without saying a word, Mrs. A. H. rubbed the banana peel, and the banana left in it, all over the boy's head.

As he struggled to get her hand off, he made the banana spread even further into his hair. Now we were laughing while his friends looked on in utter shock.

---

[7] Whor-guan-man: meaning "what's up?"

[8] The student thought she was Jamaican

"Done," she said to him. "Next time, think twice before you throw things at people, because some of us just throw it back, gat it?"

"He gat it, Miss, he *sure* gat it," another student shouted.

When Mrs. A. H. returned to the driver, he smirked and gave her thumbs up. For the remainder of the journey, everyone sat so quietly that you could have heard a pin drop.

Chapter 4

Top-Bantz

Does the title of this chapter surprise you? Remember, we're talking about Mrs. A. H. here, and in her classroom, anything was possible!

The twenty-third of February 2009 is one date that will forever be engraved in the history of St George's High School. Mrs. A. H. had come into the lesson that morning looking "happy and gay," as she would often say.

"Well, Miss, what's on? Did you win the lottery?" Lewis Paddington asked, to which Mrs. A. H. replied, "No, but soon I'm going be just as rich as one of those winners."

"Really? How?" asked Lewis again

"Well, I've just received a letter from a publisher requesting the full manuscript of my book."

"Meaning?" I asked.

"Meaning they're going to publish my book, and I know it's gonna be a best-seller in the first year of publication!"

"Wow!" We all cheered, except Adam who said, "You, Mrs. A H; wrote a book? Who's gonna read it?"

"People like you."

"Hmm, you wish."

"So you wouldn't read my book, hey?"

"Nope!"

"Why not? Just because it's not written in Chinese?"

We all gasped.

"He's not even Chinese, Miss." Said Lewis

'Really? But his eyes—"

"What's wrong with my eyes, you opaque blob!"

"Uuuuhhhh!" Lewis gasped.

At this point, we thought Mrs. A. H. would hit Adam across the face, but then she asked, "So what part of the planet did you drop from, kid?"

"He's Japanese." I said.

"Oh?!" said Mrs. A. H.

"Yeah, I'm Japanese" Adam replied sarcastically.

"*Choi*,[9] I missed that one."

"Yeah, Miss, you flopped," Lewis said.

"Yes I did. I've been flopping so much lately, and I'm not sure why."

"Well, if you want to stop being so floppy, hit the gym!" Adam said.

The whole class gasped again, expecting the worst.

To our greatest surprise, she turned round and said to Adam, "You know, kid, it's your day today. I give it to you. You win!"

---

[9] Choi is a Nigerian slang meaning "how did I miss that?"

"Really?"

"Yes indeed, Adam, you're right. I need to hit the gym, but could you kindly give me the address of the one your mother attends?"

Adam's jaw dropped, and then, as if what she'd said was perfectly reasonable, Mrs. A. H. just turned around and carried on with the lesson.

Such banter times were very few and far between, but they were always so hilarious and classic that we actually wished it happened every day. What was even more shocking was the manner in which Mrs. A. H. responded – as though it was just a normal teacher-student everyday conversation.

This brings to mind another of those occasions. We were on the playground, and Mrs. A. H. was on duty around the sports play area. As soon as we saw her, we ran towards her because we knew that if she was in the mood, we could get her to tell us a joke or just say something amusing.

Before we could reach her, she hurried towards the opposite side of the field. When we looked towards where she was walking, we noticed a little crowd had gathered. It appeared as though a fight was going on or about to start. We rushed ahead of her and met two year 7 boys fighting.

When Mrs. A. H. got there, she tried to pull the students apart without luck. One of the boys was Jonathan. It was his first month in the school, and although Mrs. A. H. had not taught him since he joined, she'd heard about how he'd been causing so much trouble in the school. He'd been permanently expelled from his previous school for pushing another child off his bike on the boy's way home. Luckily the child had a helmet on or else the accident could have been fatal.

Jonathan threw a punch at the other boy but hit Mrs. A. H. instead. That made us gasp. Mrs. A. H. took it as if nothing had happened but then reminded us about the consequences of fighting in school and that she would have to report the incident to the head of year.

Jonathan spoke to her very rudely. All of a sudden another boy came from behind and pulled at Jonathan's left arm – and it fell right to the ground!

Terribly surprised, Mrs. A. H. reached towards the arm to pick it up, but before she could, Jonathan picked it up, screaming, "Get off, you wobbly bee!"

Ignoring the abuse, she said very politely, "You don't have to be rude, Jonathan. I was only trying to help. I didn't realize you wore an artificial arm. What happened? Was it an accident, or were you born—"

Before she could complete the question, Jonathan replied, "You broke it," as he fixed the arm back on.

"Ha, amusing. Seriously, child, don't joke about such matters. Were you born that way or —"

"No, I wasn't born that way, but when I was 3 months old, my mother got so frustrated with me she threw me into the ocean, and I fought a shark, and it ate my arm."

"OK, smart mouth, enough of this nonsense. I'm sending you to Mrs. Butler at the IEU[10] for the rest of the afternoon. You're not in the right frame of mind to go to lessons for the remainder of the day."

---

[10] IEU: internal exclusion unit, or a place to have a time out.

"Well, you're not in the right frame of body to tell me what to do, you fatty neurotic sheath!"[11]

"Well, next time you have the shark fight, I hope it bites off your mouth too, you little prat!" She cursed as she walked off.

---

[11] Neurotic sheath – a fatty layer which insulates a neurone and speeds up the rate of impulse transmission.

Chapter 5

Mrs. A. H.'s Got Talent

Mrs. A. H. was in every sense the most unpredictable person we'd ever met. By "we", I mean the entire student population. It was impossible to predict what she had up her sleeve each day, but we loved it. The sheer expectation of what would happen in each lesson raised the school's attendance by a significant percentage; none of us ever missed a lesson since she started. Her teaching style brought each lesson to life for us. She was just one teacher we couldn't stay away from; like or hate her, you just wanted to be there anyway. It was like watching a live performance.

Be that as it may, we were totally unaware that Mrs. A. H. still had some hidden talents until Rachael began to sing in the lesson one day. Her singing was disrupting the lesson, so Mrs. A. H. asked her to stop, but she continued.

So Mrs. A. H. said, "You need to stop singing, Rachael, because right now, your singing is stinging my ears."

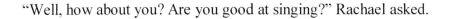

"Well, how about you? Are you good at singing?" Rachael asked.

"Yes I am."

"No you're not."

"Well, I am – take it or leave it."

"Prove it."

"What do you mean, prove it?"

"As in; sing a song right now to prove to us that you can sing."

"I don't have to prove anything to you. Get on with your work."

"You've chickened out, Miss; you can't sing." Rachael giggled.

"I can, and I'll prove it to you by getting on the St George's Got Talent Show this year."

"I dare you, Miss, and if you even get past the first stage, I'll give you my entire life's savings."

"And how much is that, darling?"

"One hundred and five pounds."

"OK, you got a deal, kid." She said and walked over to her seat to seal the bet with a handshake.

Mrs. A. H. entered the competition and surprised everyone by not just getting past the first two stages; she went on to become one of the five finalists. True to the bet, Rachael sent the money to Mrs. A. H. However, she refused to accept it. She claimed going through the competition had revived her singing talent, which had been dormant for years.

Rachael was so moved by this that she set up a Mrs. A. H. fan club. Within four hours of advertising for members, they hit their target of thirty. We were told they actually had more than one hundred applications in total.

Finally, the last day of the competition came, and it was well attended by parents and students. Mrs. A. H. wowed everyone with the song she had written as a tribute to all her students past and present. I can still clearly remember the lyrics now:

"They are the hope for our tomorrow
They are the dream that we must follow
Light the flame within their hearts
Teach them with love, and peace and truth
Show them the way; that they may follow
Save this world for the ones of tomorrow.

Visions will fade; grow dim; as they wonder
Why we destroy, pollute, kill each other
We must stop; and change our ways
Teach them with love, and peace and truth
Show them the way that they may follow
Save this world for the ones of tomorrow."

Apart from singers Mrs. A. H. and Karolina Paloskia, the other three finalists were dance groups. While the judges were counting the votes, Mrs. A. H. was asked to come back and do one more song, any song of her choice, so she sang Whitney Houston's "Greatest Love of All." It was the best version I'd ever heard, and she got a thunderous standing ovation at the end.

It was a remarkable evening, and the organizers said of the four years the competition had run, that year's attendance was more than those of all the previous years' combined. Without mincing words, they attributed the turnout to Mrs. A. H.'s participation.

Everything that happened that evening was fantastic, but the most remarkable of it all was what Mrs. A. H. did just before the results were announced.

The host, Sarah Martins, was about to announce the results when Mrs. A. H. stepped forward and put her hand up. Sarah stopped and asked, "Yes, madam? Have you got anything to say?"

"Yes, please" She replied smiling.

"Just before you announce the winner, may I make a request?"

Sarah looked at the judges. They nodded in agreement, so she handed the microphone over to Mrs. A. H. There was a moment of silence, and she began. "I'm not sure what the final results will be, but I'm sure the judges are already aware of who the winner is. So this is my request. If the actual winner turns out to be me, I'd like you to give it to Karolina. She's worked so hard for this, and I do believe that a young, talented girl like her should be given this opportunity. It would allow her develop the talent further. I'm never going to be a professional singer. I'm a teacher, and will always be, it's my life! So if it says my name, please don't read it out. Give it to my student Karolina. Thank you."

Not sure how to proceed, Sarah went to consult with the judges, and a couple of minutes later she returned to the stage. Everyone went absolutely quiet, anticipating what the judges had decided.

She cleared her throat. "I, I mean, we're totally blown away by this request, and I've never heard of such a gesture before. So it's tough to know the best way to handle this. The judges have decided to ask Karolina how she feels about the request. So, over to you, Karolina."

Karolina walked towards the microphone as everyone clapped and cheered. Then she began:

"I'm so shocked; I don't even know how to react. So, I'd just say a tremendous thank you to my beloved teacher, Mrs. A. H. You're the best teacher in the whole wide world, and we all love you *to bits*, Miss, we really do!

It would be my honour and pleasure to accept the winning trophy and prize that she has generously offered me. However, if it turns out that Mrs. A. H. really won the first place; then kindly allow her to receive the award and the ovation first. Then afterwards, she can hand it over to me. Thank you."

Everyone cheered and clapped as she walked off the stage.

Then Sarah came back on stage and said, "Wow! This is one

night that we'll all remember for as long as we live. What a remarkable night this has been. It's just awesome!"

Then, looking at the results list she'd been handed, she carried on: "As this has been a night of surprises, I shall add one more by changing the order in which we typically announce results. So, rather than go from the fifth to the first position, I shall call out the winners from the first position. So, the winner of the 2010 St. George's Got Talent is" – *(followed by a 3-second pause)* – "Mrs. A. H.!" It was such an emotional night, and everyone was on their feet as Mrs. A. H. stepped forward to receive the trophy. She then walked over to Karolina and handed her the trophy.

And as she did that, the members of *Club A. H.* ran onto the stage and put on a brilliant dance performance to The Black-Eyed Peas' "Tonight's Gonna Be a Good Night." It was simply terrific!

We later found out Rachael had secretly planned to do this if Mrs. A. H. did win the competition.

Chapter 6

Trust Me, Mrs. A. H.'s Psychic Too!

One day Mrs. A. H. gave five of us a lunch detention because we failed to hand in our homework after two reminders. This made us worried because we'd heard that her detention sessions were very weird. For example, one person said she made him sharpen 150 pencils that were so small; it took them about two and a half minutes to successfully sharpen each one. Another said she made his group read out lines from some medieval books written in Old English about some old medical practices like bloodletting and the like. Another told me she made a group of year 9 boys cry by instructing them to carry out a certain 'science practical', which involved lifting heavy blocks or boxes of books from one end of the room to the other.

No one could predict what she would require them to do, but you could be certain it would be morbid and strange. Everyone dreaded getting a detention from her.

So as we walked into the room that morning and saw her smiling, we were kind of relieved that our sanction may not be too bad after all. We were right, in a way.

As we settled into our seats, Simon said, "Miss, what's *guan*?" Simon was a year 7 boy. He'd been asked to come into Mrs. A. H.'s room for his detention because his teacher had something else to do.

To his question, she replied, "I just remembered a funny experience I had two years ago when my friend asked me to go attend her daughter's stay-and-play time. I'm going to share that story with you."

"Great, I like stories," Simon said.

We all looked at him with pity and wished he would just

shut up and not get us all into more trouble with his sarcasm. Luckily for us, Mrs. A. H. just ignored him and carried on.

"My friend's daughter, Millie, was in year 2 at the time, and the reason her mum asked me this favour was because she knew my school had been temporarily closed due to a gas leak in one of science labs. Please do not ask me to explain how or why the gas leaked because I don't know.

"So I went into this classroom with some twenty-five 7-year-olds, and for the first twenty minutes, it was so boring because all we did was move from one play area to another, sitting on chairs so small I actually felt like a Lilliputian from Jonathan Swift's *Gulliver's Travels*.

"Then it was time for parent showcase. My friend did not warn me, so I hadn't prepared for this. I wasn't worried though, because it was voluntary, so I didn't have to do anything.

"After Millie's teacher announced what the session was all about, she asked who had anything to showcase. One boy put his hand up, and a woman stood up and read out a very long, boring poem. Halfway through the reading, my mind completely wandered off, and only came to when everyone began to clap. *Thank God!* I thought, and I sighed.

"Then the teacher asked, 'Who's next?' To my greatest shock, Millie put her hand up. I immediately reached out to pull her hand down, but alas, everyone was clapping and looking at me, so I had to stop.

"I reluctantly got up, and as I stood in front looking at these bright, innocent faces, I heard a voice within me say, *C'mon, now, don't disappoint them, give it your best shot.* To which I replied to myself, *But I'm not prepared for this and—*

"Before I could complete the protest in my head, my lips began to move, and I heard my myself say, 'One day, in a very far away country in Africa ...' As soon as I said Africa, every pair of eyes in the room lit up and pierced through me in a way that I knew I just had to make this worth their while.

"There lived a little girl called Sonia. She was a brilliant girl and attended a very expensive private school because her parents were really rich. They also lived in one of the posh areas in the city of Lagos.

"One day, Sonia went to her school library and saw this magic book titled *Magic It.* 'Huh?' Sonia said, *Magic It*? I'm definitely gonna borrow this book.'

"'No you won't,' a voice said from behind her. It was her older sister, Thalisha.

"Who's gonna stop me, you? *He-he*!" Sonia giggled as she dashed out of the library tightly clasping the book.

"That night when Sonia got home, she locked herself up in her room and began to read the magic book. She read all night, and unknown to Thalisha, Sonia was also practicing some of the magic on the things in their room.

"Thalisha realized Sonia was practicing magic because as soon as she opened her eyes, the light immediately came on. 'What? Who did that?' Thalisha asked in surprise, and then the lights went off again.

"'*Aaaaahhhhh!*' Thalisha screamed as she ran out of the room shouting, 'Monster! Monster! Muuum, there's a monster in our room!'

"'Come on, Thalisha, monsters aren't real. You must have had a nightmare, dear. And I've told you that any time you have a nightmare, just say a little prayer to the Father in Jesus' name and all will be well, OK?' her mother said from the living room.

"In frustration, Thalisha went back to her room and warned Sonia to stop reading the magic book and trying to practice any of the magic in that book or else she would report to their mother.

"Sonia replied, 'OK, OK, madam-senior-sister-Thalisha. Tomorrow I shall return the book, and we will forget this ever happened.'

"Thalisha did forget about it, believing it would be the end of Sonia and her magic book. But for Sonia, the excitement of seeing Thalisha run out of the room in panic was so thrilling that she was determined to try out some more of the magic. She had lied that she would return the book, for fear of being told off by their mother.

"The following day, their cousins Billy and Tobi came to visit. As they sat doing some Math work in the living room, they suddenly saw Sonia walking down the stairs smiling.

"Thalisha looked at Sonia and asked, 'Why are you smiling like that anyway? What's so funny?'

"Sonia replied, 'Well, big sister, I shall demonstrate to you what's funny in a minute – watch me. Now, where's my balloon mummy bought for my sixth birthday last Monday?'

"'It's hanging on there,' Thalisha said, pointing towards the balloon.

"Then Sonia turned around to face the balloon and, pointing her finger, began to say some really weird incantations.

"All of a sudden she said, 'I command you, number six to turn into number seven and come alive. I command you to *transform, transform, transfoooorrrm*!'

"To everyone's amazement, the balloon changed into the figure seven and began to walk towards them.

"All the children began to scream.

"Thalisha shouted at Sonia to stop the magic, but Sonia just stood there laughing her head off.

"The monster seven started to chase the boys. Billy jumped out the window, shouting, in a bid to escape the monster.

"As Tobi tried to run, his leg got caught by a rope, so he shouted, 'Billy! Billy! My brother, please wait for me! Wait for me!'

But Billy replied, 'Brother? There's nothing like brother

right now. Not when I've got a monster to run away from –
everyone for himself, *fam*!'

"By this time their aunt Vicky opened the front door, and
as soon as she saw the monster seven, she too began to run.

"Thalisha said, 'Aunty Vicky, Demi's upstairs. Can you get
her, please?'

"Aunty Vicky replied, 'Ah, upstairs? I can't go there now.
Oh, I'm scared.'

"'But Aunty Vicky, you're supposed to be taking care of us. Go and rescue Demi.'

"To which Vicky replied, 'What, me, take care? Not when there's a monster around. Jesus is taking care of us, and I'm not moving an inch. Demi will be okay – the angels are there with her.' She ran away as fast as she could.

"Just then they saw Demi walking down the stairs holding the magic book. Unknown to them all, while they were all downstairs, Demi woke up, found the book, and began reading it from where Sonia had left off. She'd read the page on how to reverse the magic; they were a series of weird words.

"As Demi came downstairs, the monster seven started chasing after her, but Demi stretched out her hand and shouted, 'No, monster, no! I now command you to return back to normal.' She read out these gibberish sounding magical words – '*agiloli, agiloli, agiloli!*' – and all of a sudden, the monster seven stopped, changed back into the number six birthday balloon, and hung back up where it had been before.

"'Pheeew!' Thalisha screamed.

"Just then, Billy heard his older brother, Bartholomew, calling his name and shaking him vigorously.

"When he opened his eyes, Bartholomew had a quizzical look on his face and said, 'What's the matter with you, shouting in your sleep like that?'

"Tobi replied, 'Oh my God, so it was just a dream then?'

"The end."

"And how is that funny, Miss?" Adam asked.

To which Mrs. A. H. replied, "Well, it's not, but it's ingenious because I made that up on the spot. I think I'm a genius."

"Hmm. So how many people clapped at the end?" Adam asked.

"Clapped? None. Instead, all the adults gawped at me in amazement. While the children, bless them, had such shock on their faces that their thoughts about me naturally dovetailed into my mind. They were saying, 'You're the monster'."

"So what did you do?" questioned Adam

"I picked up my bag and walked out of the room."

This teacher is so weird, I thought as she turned around to write something on the board, and at that very moment, she turned round, looked straight into my eyes, and said, "Aha, I heard that!"

"Aaahhh!" I screamed as I ran out of the classroom; detention over.

Chapter 7

I Hate PE

At the end of that school day, I was so sure I wouldn't be in school the following morning, but I actually did attend. We didn't have any lessons with Mrs. A. H. on Thursdays because she covered PE all day. She told us that Thursdays were her worst days of the week because she hated PE lessons. Apart from that, she said she had one particular group with some very badly behaved boys. Although she had several ways of keeping them in line, she confessed that she felt terribly exhausted after those lessons.

My next-door neighbour Cody was one of the students in that particular year group. He said she told them that their group was the most challenging of all classes she'd ever taught. Cody came home with lots of stories about those lessons, and according to him, they actually looked forward to them because just like I could testify to, Mrs. A. H. was indeed unpredictable. One was never certain what strategy she would cook up to keep the disruptive students in line or to make the lazy ones work to the best of their abilities.

]He told me what their very first PE lesson with Mrs. A. H. was like. She had come into that room wearing everyday clothes, which surprised the students, so they tried to explain how that particular lesson was a double and that they were doing athletics.

She replied, "And so what?"

"But, Miss, if we're doing athletics, surely you wouldn't be able to run in those clothes," Oliver said.

"And who said I was going to run, eh, who said?"

"But, Miss, every PE teacher runs with their students." Said Oliver

"Well, you just met a different one. I don't do running."

"No?" asked Oliver, surprised.

"No. I don't do running, walking, jumping, jogging – nothing!"

"Well then, if you don't do it, we wouldn't either!" Oliver said.

"OK kid, we'll see about that!" She turned round to face the rest of the class and ordered, "C'mon, y'all, get your butts off *da* chair and get going – out to the field right now. Let's go!"

Once the students got outside, they mocked about rather than line up and get ready for the warm-up. Some were leaning against the wall while others just stood in groups, chatting.

It was a particularly freezing winter morning, and Mrs. A. H. was not in any mood to persuade these youngsters with words; she knew that wouldn't work but decided to try it anyway, so she politely said, "Could everyone line up here, please?"

No one responded, so she raised her hand to get everyone's attention and said, "Ye lads and lasses need to begin your warm-up now; you're wasting time. For those of you still in uniform, you need to go put your PE kit on, quick."

"Why don't you start the warm-up session, Miss? You're the teacher, aren't you?" one of the boys asked, laughing.

"Are you kidding me, kid? Start the warm-up session? How can I? Have you seen me lately? Take another look; I am big. Massive, you know, *fat*. The last time I walked to school, it took me an hour even though I only live two miles down the road."

Everyone burst into laughter.

"Well, you can laugh all you like. I see nothing funny in this, and it's the truth. I don't do sports. I hate sports, I hate PE. In fact, I hate PE so much that I actually hate words that begin with the letters *p and e*. For example, I don't like pets, I never use pegs, I have never bought petrol, and I loathe penguins. Peanuts give you gas, peas are disgusting – you just name it, I hate anything that begins with PE!"

"Miss, you're so weird!" said Cody.

"That's my middle name, darling. Now, will you all get in line? Or else I'll make you."

"Make us then, Miss," said some students.

"OK, guys, you asked for it!" she shouted as she dashed off into the direction of the changing rooms.

In a flash she returned, fully changed into a jogging suit, her shoes swapped for a pair of black trainers. Before we could recover from her change of outfit, she pulled out a very long garden hosepipe and began to squirt cold water on everyone.

In a bid to dodge the bitterly cold water, everyone took off running, while she stood there wearing a grin of satisfaction across her face. She kept chasing them all round until they got to the end of the field. Allowing them just a few minutes to catch their breath, she started squirting the water again. The students took off running back, many of them swearing and calling her all sorts of names.

Being who she was, she couldn't care less; the abuse meant nothing to her as long as she got the students doing her bidding!

When I shared this story with my classmates, one of them told me she did something similar to her brother's class. These were year 11 students who were particularly lazy. My cousin Ethan was in that class. As Ethan later told me, she had on one occasion taken them to the basketball cage for practice as they had a match the following day. These boys were no doubt superb at basketball, and the school they were competing against was nowhere near them in terms of ability and achievement. This made the boys complacent. However, the head of the PE insisted they practiced like never before. He had heard about the rival school's determination to win the trophy at all cost. Their head teacher had put an irresistible price to the trophy.

When Mrs. A. H. tried to explain this to the boys, they totally ignored her, and one of them reminded her that she knew nothing about basketball so she couldn't really umpire their game. When she insisted on their practicing regardless, the boys began to mock about and laugh at her.

One of them challenged her and said, "*Yo*, Miss, if you can bounce this ball from one end of the cage to the other, then we'll all play like mad."

This made her so angry that she replied, "For the very last time, I'm warning you, lads, go on and start practicing or else you wouldn't like the consequences of your actions. I warn you!"

"What would you do, spray us with cold water like you did to some students last time?" asked Ethan.

"Sorry, there's neither water nor hosepipe about, sorry!" another boy mocked, and they all laughed even more.

To everyone's surprise, Mrs. A. H. pulled out some very strange-looking sewage tanker hosepipe from a bag. She began to shoot out tennis balls.

The first boy who got hit by a ball screamed, rigorously rubbing the spot to ease the pain. Then she fired another one and another.

The boys immediately picked up the basketball and began practicing in frenzy. As they dashed from one end of the cage to the other, bouncing the ball and aiming for the basket, she stood in one corner of the cage, pointing the hosepipe at them, giggling. She did not leave that position or put the hosepipe down until the bell rang for a change of lessons.

The boys were very tired at the end of it, but strangely felt good about their practice. As expected, they won the trophy – albeit by a hair's breadth. They all agreed that if they hadn't practiced the day before, they would have easily lost the match to the rival school. So, once again, our crazy Mrs. A. H. saved the day!

Chapter 8

Her Prom Story

To reward her for her effort towards helping them win the trophy, they invited Mrs. A. H. as a special guest to their prom. To everyone's surprise she turned down the offer, saying she had very strong reasons for not attending proms. The year 11 students who were really excited about having her at their prom tried to get her to explain, but she refused.

When I heard about it, I decided to ask her myself.

So on this particular day, I made sure I completed all my work on time and took a very active part in the lesson, and when she asked for a volunteer to go fetch some books from the science annex block, I put my hand up.

As I walked into the classroom clasping the book against my chest, she looked at me quizzically and said, "*Steve*, I strongly believe there's a reason you're extra kind to me today, right?"

The question threw me off balance, but she was right, as always. "You psychic toad brain," I said under my breath, praying she didn't hear me. Then, with a fake smile, I replied, "In fact, Miss, there is."

"Awww!" Adam said.

"Shut up, you plum head," was my response to Adam's teasing, and then to Mrs. A. H., I asked, "Why do you hate proms, Miss?"

"Because I never had one."

"Really? Why not?"

"Well, it's a long story, which I'd rather not share."

"Oh, please, Miss, tell us; we want to hear it."

"Hmmm." She thought for a while, rolling her eyes, and then said, "Well, if you come back at lunchtime today, I'll tell you."

"OK then, Miss." I said.

At lunchtime I went to hear the story, accompanied by three of my friends.

The story went thus:

Apparently, Mrs. A. H. was a stubborn brat in secondary school. She had a group of friends who were really badly behaved and were constantly in trouble with the school authority. Their misbehaviour reached its breaking point when one of them set the deputy head teacher's computer bag on fire. Luckily it was made of very sturdy leather, so before it could burn through, the fire alarm went off, and the contents of the bag were rescued.

According to Mrs. A. H., she knew nothing about this particular incident so felt the head teacher's decision to punish her along with her friends was most unfair.

So Mrs. A. H got the entire year 11 students to sign a petition against the school for being unfair in their administration of justice.

This letter of protest became counterproductive because when the school's governing body received the letter, they summoned the head teacher. After looking through the record of the terrible things these students had done, the governing body cancelled the prom for that year. This, they said, was to serve as a deterrent to other students that such level of bad behaviour would never be tolerated at the Sacred Heart Catholic School.

Mrs. A. H. said it was a particularly painful experience for all the students because they had worked extra hard to get the prom subsidized by a local Superstores by 80 per cent.

As if cancelling the event wasn't bad enough, the teachers decided to use the opportunity for a teachers' night out! All they needed to do was contribute money to pay back the students' 20 per cent contribution so that they could attend their "prom" instead.

Mrs. A. H. said this wound her up so much that she masterminded the plan to disrupt the so-called teachers' night out.

"How could the teachers ever think of such an evil thing?"

she asked rhetorically between clenched teeth. One could tell she still felt the pain. Without actually giving the details of how she pulled it off, she and her friends – or should I say partners in crime – ruined the evening for the teachers by spiking their desserts and increasing the alcohol contents of their drinks.

The following morning, many of the teachers called in sick, and those who showed up looked totally stoned and hammered. She said it was by far the funniest day of her secondary school days.

When Mrs. A. H. got to the end of that story, an idea crept into my head: *I think I should write a book about this crazy teacher, outlining her day-to-day activities since she became my science teacher.*

I was so excited about this idea that I didn't hear myself say, "Miss, so how old are you?"

She turned round and gave me that stare, which only meant one thing: drop that subject now or else! So I did. I dropped it right there and then.

However, the idea of writing a book about her had been so engraved in my subconscious that I was convinced that nothing, not even "sixty-six mad-men"[12] (as Mrs. A. H. would say), could stop me.

I couldn't at that moment see the possibility of achieving the target, but at the same time, I couldn't imagine anything big enough to stop me.

---

[12] This is one of Mrs. A.H's weird phrases

Chapter 9

The Bag Swap

As I hurried towards the bus stop that evening, an idea dropped in my mind. *What if I trailed Mrs. A. H. to her house? Yes, what if I did? Then I could study her movements to find clues that would enable me write an excellent story about her.*

But a voice within me counseled: *Surely that would be stalking, and, my dear boy, stalking is a crime in this country, remember?* So, I reconsidered. Yeah, that would be stalking, but … Before I could complete the thought, my bus pulled up, and I got on. Momentarily breaking my line of thought, I showed the driver my bus pass and sat at the rear; the bus was practically empty.

I was famished, so I rummaged through my bag for the Galaxy chocolate bar I'd reserved from my lunch pack. But the inside of my bag felt really weird; I thought I felt something like a pair of scissors. *What?* I thought. I took another look, and it dawned on me; I had the wrong bag. *Oh, bullocks! Now I have to go back to school because my bag has my house keys in it.*

My parents were away on some training course, and my uncle, who was looking after me, was working late that day. I felt so angry that I nearly used a really terrible swear word, but I restrained myself and pushed hard on the stop button instead. It was so loud and long that the bus driver gave me evils as I walked past him.

"Buzz off!" I whispered angrily as I stepped off the bus, trying at the same time to work out in my head how and where I had mixed up the bags. I couldn't tell whose bag I had from just looking at it, so I took another look inside to recall if anyone else had the same Nike bag as mine.

Then I remembered – Damian Burgess. But how did his bag get mixed up with mine? Or was this just the handiwork of some of those *plum heads* I call classmates? I wasn't finding this prank funny at all!

"Hello, Steve!" I jumped at the sound of the voice that just called my name.

"Ahh…Miss! Wow, you scared me!"

"Ha-ha" She laughed and said, "Yeah, I know I did, I always do. Anyway, what's the matter? Why were you mumbling to yourself?"

"Mumbling? Really? I didn't realize my lips were moving."

"Well, they were. So, what's the matter?"

"I have to go back to school to find my bag. I mistakenly took the wrong one."

"Oh dear!" she said, laughing again.

"But, Miss, it's not funny."

"Sorry, I know it's not, but it's just that … ha-ha-ha, I'm really sorry, but I can't help it! He-he-he. You know, I'm very sure one of your friends played a fast one on you. Oh, you youngsters. You're all the same, from generation to generation. But why go back to school when you could actually pick it up tomorrow? And how would you know if the person who's got yours is still in school?"

"Well, it's got my house keys in it."

"Now, that's serious. Are your parents working late or something?"

I explained the situation to her. Then she said I should go to School and tell the receptionist to contact Damien's parents.

Taking a look at her watch, she added, "You know what? You go to school, and I'll go pick up my car and meet you there in about five minutes."

"Really, are you sure Miss?"

"Yes. I only live down the road, number fifty-eight on the first street on your left; off St David's Road. If Damien's parents can't bring the keys to school tonight, I'll drive to theirs to get them for you."

"Would you do that, Miss?"

"Oh yeah, it's a small thing. It's all part of my job."

"No, I disagree with you on that, Miss. This is not part of your job. This is purely an angelic gesture, and I truly appreciate it, honestly."

As she walked off, I thought, *Surely no one would believe this part of my story. Mrs. A. H. did not just give me her home address and offered to help me find my keys. This is beyond fiction ... what? I even can't believe it.*

As I walked towards the school churning these things over in my mind, I became much more determined to write that book.

When I arrived at the school, the receptionist informed me that Damien had returned my bag because he found my keys in it. He wasn't able to wait so he said he would pick his up the following day.

Just then Mrs. A. H. arrived. She was happy that I'd found my keys. Naturally, I walked her to her car, restating my appreciation for her care and concern. She said it was fine, got into her car, and drove off.

As I turned to walk away, I noticed on the spot where she'd

parked her car something that looked like a notepad. I walked over, picked it up, and opened it.

It was her diary!

Chapter 10

The Changes

Totally propelled by my natural reflexes, I began to walk towards the reception, intending to hand it over, but then I stopped as I heard that voice within me say: *Hang on a minute. Mrs. A. H.'s diary. Isn't that just what you need to find out all the tiny, juicy secrets about this woman that would make your story a delight to read by every student at St George's High?*

Yeah, that's right you know! I thought. *I shall take this diary home, copy all the pages, and then come into school very early the following day and drop it off in a place where the receptionist would see it and give it back to her. But hold on. What if someone sees me on the CCTV camera? Mrs. A. H. may want to find out how her diary got to the reception – she's weird like that. I wouldn't do that. Instead, I shall put it in the post first thing tomorrow morning. Yes, that's what I'll do.*

I hardly had any sleep that night because as soon as I read the very first entry, I was hooked, and I couldn't drop it until I got to the last page. All of the questions that I had about this crazy teacher became clear to me. She had her life laid out in the pages of that diary. She even had lots and lots of loose sheets stapled to some pages of the diary wherever she needed to write more than the diary page could hold. If I were to outline the content of the diary, it would be a book on its own, so I focused on the mysteries I unraveled as I read through.

She began each entry with the date and DD, which I guessed meant *Dear Diary*. Before I explain what I discovered, let me backtrack a bit and pick up the story from the beginning of the new Mrs. A. H.

About sixteen months after Mrs. A. H. began teaching at our school, we noticed some changes in her behaviour and general attitude. For example, she became a lot calmer in lessons, shouted less at disruptive students, gave fewer detentions, and laughed a lot more. I mean genuine laughter, unlike the sarcastic, tormenting one we'd endured for months.

Apart from all that, she began to lose weight. At first we noticed she was always coming into school sweating, saying that she just felt like walking to school. She gradually progressed to running and taking more interest in PE lessons. Ethan even said the entire class was shocked that she was actually participating. By the second week it was so obvious that she was on some sort of weight-loss program, but no one dared ask.

Her wardrobe began to change. She wore dresses more often and high-heeled shoes rather than her usual plimpsoles.

Now, to the entries in her dairies, she had written nothing but tales of woe from her first day at St George's High School. She wrote everything about her classes and all the fun she was having keeping the students in line.

Hmm, I thought. *So I was right on that one. Mrs. A. H. did derive pleasure from* torturing *us; OMD,*[13] *what a crazy woman!*

However, she had a reason really, because when she took over our class, we were tough to handle. She thus became the only teacher after many who could successfully put the group in check and working to potential. No one can take that from her.

I also found out that she wasn't married; she just used the "Mrs." title because she felt it made students respect teachers more.

However, from round about the same time we began to see those changes in her, her diary entries changed. From then on until the day before I found the diary, she wrote absolutely nothing about St. George's High. She had a new focus, a new reason for living, something to talk about all day long: the stranger she secretly admired!

---

[13] OMD: oh my days.

Chapter 11

Her Diaries

The highlight of her diaries included the following:

21.03

DD,

I firmly believe I've found the one! OMG, he's so handsome! I just can't take my mind off him, OMG! Funny enough, though, I don't even know his name ⋯ lol!

23.03

DD,

You wouldn't believe who I saw at Tesco today. It was him! He didn't see me though; I spied him through the shelves. At one point he walked past me and I nearly stopped breathing, but I pulled myself together and prayed he would take notice of me and say hello. OMG, what a dude he is; j-e-e-e-e-z!!

03.04

DD,

Do you know it's been ten days? *Ten* whole days, and I haven't seen him anywhere! Please don't tell me he's left the city or that he was just visiting or something. I was so sure he worked in one of the offices at the Shield Hall in the City Centre. I trailed him there last week. But now he's vanished! I think I'm gonna die, I'm just gonna ··· but wait, die? No way, God forbid. I wouldn't die; I'll go hunting for him instead. Yes, that's what I'm gonna do – but hunt for him where?! Just where?!

08.04

DD,

Yippee, yippee, yeah! I've found him! I found him!! And I'm dancing, and dancing!

He's still in town. Gosh, I'm so happy! Oh God, please let him notice me when we next meet. God, pleassssse ⋯ I'm on my knees!!

10.04

DD,

Today, something terrible happened to me. Remember my friend Yolanda, the skinny one with the massive head and thick lips? She said it would be a splendid idea if I went swimming because swimming made one burn fat quicker and strengthen all body muscles.

So I went swimming. As soon as I walked through the swimming pool door, I saw him, and he was totally topless! My heart skipped three beats, but before I could recover, he jumped into the pool! I jumped in too, my mind totally blank. I didn't know what I was doing.

Then, at that instant it occurred to me: *Pretend you're drowning, so he can come and rescue you.* So I began to fake drowning, but to my greatest surprise this guy jumped out of the pool and pulled at some red button on the wall. He set off the alarm.

Oh my days! But I couldn't stop the drama then; I'd gone too far. I carried on "drowning" and then this very skinny man who was standing nearby jumped into the pool to rescue me. You know what? I was so angry that I nearly drowned him. I made sure I taught him a lesson never to attempt to rescue a fat woman again.

Uhhh, but that was so close!

11.04

DD,

Bored stiff, thinking and dreaming of him all day, I decided to try the swimming pool again. I swam and swam until my eyes were bloodshot from the chlorinated water, but Mr Handsome did not show up! Oh God, what am I going to do? "Where are you, my handsome, where are you?!"

17.04

DD,

I feel like not doing anything right now, you know? Because I'm so, so sad!

Well, Mr Pearson, the geography teacher, asked if I could join him today on the trip to the school down the road, Queen Elizabeth II Senior School. He had to take the year 7 students for a lecture of some sort. I agreed. It all went smoothly until we had to go for lunch; as I stood waiting to be served, who did I notice? That's right, it was him. Before I could think up a plan to finally say hello to him, this very pretty, skinny girl in a hot skirt walked up to him and started chatting him up! What the heck!! I felt like hitting her across the face! I was so green with envy as he laughed at everything she said! I couldn't eat anything. OMG! The sight of him and that girl just made me lose my appetite.

You know, my plan was to lose a pound a day, but after seeing that skinny Halloween witch trying to get the attention of my man, I decided to make it three a day. I shall run ten to fifteen miles every evening too, until I hit my target weight of dress size twelve! *Rubbish!*

Who the *hec* does she think she is? Just who? I'm so, so angry right now as I write this! DD, you have no idea how I actually feel right now; how could you? You're not even a living thing. Oh God, help me, I think I'm losing my sanity!

Mr Handsome didn't show up! Oh God, what am I going to do? Where are you, my handsome? Where are you?

22.05

DD,

I've been very upset but really busy for the last two weeks. I haven't written anything since because I wasn't in the mood for talking. However, I'm doing great with the weight loss. In fact, I bought a top today at Primark that I was sure wouldn't fit me, especially my arms. But you wouldn't believe it ⋯ it was too big! For the first time in the one hundred years of my life (it feels like that), a top was too large for me! I was so excited to try the next size down, and it fit, so I'm now officially a size eighteen – three dress sizes down.

Regarding Mr Handsome, I'm also making progress on that project. At least I now know his name is Lucas, and he is Mauritian. I also know he's a teacher at the Queen Elizabeth II Senior School. Let me confess: I've been dreaming so much about him that he just seems to turn up everywhere I go! Oohh! I'm longing for this guy more and more each day, yet he doesn't even know I exist! I terribly need help and urgently, too.

30.05

DD,

Today, I finally got the courage to drop a hint about Lucas to Yolanda. She was so happy for me, and when I confessed to her that I was pushed to stalking him, she told me to nip the idea in the bud but promised to find out all about him for me. So right now, Yolanda, you're the most beautiful person in the world as far as I'm concerned. You're officially the BFF of the year!

From then on, Mrs. A. H. had so many lovely entries in her diary about "my Lucas," as she called him. Yolanda was doing such a great job finding out about him, and to Mrs. A. H.'s relief, the "skinny witch" was no threat at all as she was Lucas's NQT[14] mentee.

Everything ran smoothly for weeks, and Yolanda was frantically seeking ways to bring Lucas and Christine (Mrs.. A. H.'s first name) together, but then something cropped up. Yolanda had to travel out of the country for four weeks. It was an official assignment.

As she explained in her diary, she nearly passed out when she heard the news. This threw her into depression (which she perfectly concealed at school because apart from the notes in her diary, she was just the same person to all of us).

It was on the fifth day of Yolanda's absence that I found the dairy. Mrs. A. H. had written this entry:

---

[14] NQT Newly Qualified Teacher

02.06

DD,

I feel so terrible again today. This is only day four of the four weeks before my helper/angel, Yolanda, returns to the country. Four whole weeks! I'm gonna die, I just know it. I'm dying because I can't put this plan of getting hooked with Lucas on hold for four weeks! What if he meets someone in that time? What if he leaves the country? What if he suddenly gets a job in Afghanistan? What if? What if … OMG! I need Yolanda back in the UK right now! What's worse is, she's not flipping picking her phone calls or responding to messages on FB. Oh yes, I know it, I'm just gonna die! Oh help me, God, help me!

Chapter 12

The Perfect Plan

As I read those words, I could almost feel the desperation of her soul. So, I decided to place the matter before my cousin Ethan. After days of deliberation, we came up with a plan.

Ethan and I did some research and discovered that Lucas, surnamed Dawson, was a Math teacher at the Elizabeth II Senior School. When we asked, we found a friend of ours who's Cousin John attended that school. We made him our *link-man*.

John and two of his mates gave us the valid pieces of information we needed to successfully execute our plan. It took us a few weeks, but we achieved the first part. We successfully introduced Mrs. A. H. To Lucas; her picture that is.

We managed to convince Lucas to go along with our plan.

Our meeting was a fascinating and quick one because just one look at Mrs. A. H.'s photo, he liked her. He asked for the full plan.

Before, explaining, I confessed that I'd found out about Mrs. A.H.'s crush on him from reading her dairy. He rebuked me for doing that saying it was an invasion of her privacy. I said I was really very sorry and would never do such a thing again. He said it was OK but that he would take the matter up personally from there. *Hmm, talk about love at first sight!* We were impressed but managed to convince him against the idea; we were enjoying this so much, that his idea would have ruined our plans.

Let me also pause to add that at this point, Mrs. A. H. looked nearly half her former size – impressive, right? Well, that's the power of love.

When we asked Lucas about the 'skinny girl' that Mrs. A. H. had believed to be his girlfriend, he laughed and gave us an explanation that confirmed what Yolanda already found out.

All of that sorted, we decided to take the plan to the next level, which was to get Lucas to send love notes to Mrs. A. H. As expected, the love notes totally annoyed Mrs. A. H. She came to lesson every day moaning about how some *silly-fellow* had been sending stupid love notes to her. Adding that if only this "idiot" knew how much she hated him, he would run very far from her. To make matters worse, we sent a picture (not Lucas') with one of the notes. This just made her "go completely *fâché*[15]," if I may borrow one of her phrases.

The notes and flowers carried on while we tried to encourage her to give the person a chance, but she wouldn't hear of it, so we were thinking of the next line of action and needed to come up with something really fast because Lucas was getting very impatient. Then the golden moment came one morning when Mrs. A. H. announced that it was going to be her birthday.

Bingo! I thought. *This is it! This is so definitely it! We shall organize a surprise birthday party for her and present Lucas as the special birthday gift. Perfect! But how shall we ensure that she realizes that Lucas had been sending the notes and accept his proposal?*

---

[15] *fâché*- in French meaning angry

The answers wouldn't form in my head, so I decided to discuss it with Ethan. After some two hours of thinking and weighing several options, Ethan concluded we needed Mr Oakley on board.

We had a meeting with the head teacher and explained everything to him. He readily bought into the idea and added that our explanation had helped clarify many of the questions he had regarding Mrs. A. H.'s change in appearance. The head teacher decided he would direct Mrs. A. H. to come and do a special duty in school on the evening of her birthday. He would tell her that some African Gospel Choir had requested to use the school hall for a fundraising event for Red Nose day.

Everyone knew Mrs. A. H. spoke very passionately about things like that. It worked! She told Mr Oakley that it would be a worthwhile way to spend the evening of her birthday as she had made no plans for the evening.

As we heaved a sigh of relief on that aspect, something else came up: Mrs.. Watts was taken to hospital. She was scheduled to run the much talked about assembly of the year. This raised a lot of concern among staff, students, and parents. This assembly was one of the highlights of the year at our school.

So the news that Mrs. A. H. had volunteered to run the assembly came with mixed feelings. On one hand, we liked the idea of her running it, but on the other, we feared she might swap it with attending the fundraising event. She was unpredictable like that, you know?

It was becoming like a never-ending hurdle race: a jump over one hurdle only brings one nearer the next.

Chapter 13

The Power of Choice

It was with much fear and trepidation that we took our seats in the hall that morning. Eagerly awaiting the all-important assembly to begin. A million thoughts must have flash through my mind each minute. This assembly was very special because it was the last one for the year. In a way, it ushered in the summer holidays.

As it was customary at St George's High, the first NQT to arrive at the school ran it. This NQT had the whole year to prepare for it, and there was generally a lot of hullabaloo about it all year long. It was always spectacular.

As it turned out this year, the lot fell on Mrs. Judith Watts from the English department. However, by mid-April Mrs. Watts took ill. Within a few weeks it was announced that she was pregnant. By the last week of June, she had to go into hospital for a two-week monitoring period.

She was so determined to deliver this assembly, but two days after her return, and just forty-eight hours to the event, she had to be taken to hospital again. This threw the school management into a state of panic, wondering how they could convince any other teacher to step in for Mrs. Watts at such short notice – and most importantly, deliver an assembly good enough to meet everyone's expectation.

When Mrs. A.H. volunteered, management was relieved but unsure if she could run it well, considering she only had twenty-four hours to prepare. As she stepped onto the podium that morning, I had doubts she would deliver an assembly speech comparable to previous ones but secretly prayed that she hadn't swapped this for the Saturday event … and then her voice joggled me back to reality as she cleared her throat and began.

"I'm pleased to stand before you all to deliver this assembly this morning. After I had sent an email to Mr Oakley volunteering to step in for Mrs. Watts, fear and confusion gripped me. I didn't know exactly what to talk about. As it was such short notice, I couldn't create a PowerPoint presentation. My PC skills are not that rudimentary, so I could have put something together, but as you all know, it's been a manic term for all of us, so my apologies.

"Last night I thought long and hard about what would be a good topic at this time of the year, and I decided to tell a true story: my story.

"As a young girl growing up in Africa in the seventies, the last day of term was always special because that was the day we got our final reports. We found out how well we'd performed in the exam and learned whether we'd been promoted to the next higher class. You see, promotion from year to year wasn't automatic; whoever failed to meet the pass mark for the core subjects repeated a whole year. I was always happy because I did very well in academics. I had to; it was the only source of happiness and hope I had back then.

"At age 11, I left my parents to live with my aunty in the big city; she was a primary school teacher. My parents thought living with her would afford me the opportunity to attend a good school and get a good education. For my parents, education was our only way out of the abject poverty we were in.

"I did get a good education but under adverse conditions of terrible abuse. I was abused physically, mentally, and psychologically.

"My auntie's husband was a hopeless drunk. He couldn't keep a job and couldn't stand up to my auntie. I was young, helpless, and fat, so he found me an easy vent for his frustrations. He'd smack me and call me *"mouka-foam"*[16] several times a day. He'd force me to wash the clothes he'd been sick on.

"This and the excessive house chores made me late to school every day, and because my uniform and shoes had holes in them, I got mocked by many students.

"The only thing that gave me joy was the praise and commendations I got from my teachers for excellent work in all school subjects.

"On the day I turned 13, I decided to put an end to the

---

[16] Mouka Foam is a mattress company in Africa that makes very thick, soft mattresses. Calling someone "mouka-foam" was a derogatory way of saying the person was fat and floppy.

abuse from my uncle and chose to defend myself. So on this faithful day, as he staggered into my room, intending to hit me as usual, I threw a very massive book at him, which caught him right across the face. He was so shocked and hurt that he ran out of the room cursing and swearing that he would kill me.

"I ran out of the house and slept in the churchyard for six nights. I met another runaway girl who had been sleeping there for months. She was wild and magnificent at karate. She taught me some karate moves, and on the seventh day of taking intensive lessons, I returned home.

"My auntie was so nonchalant that she didn't even ask where I had been. As I walked past my uncle, I paused and gave him a stern look that made him shake his head and look away. From that day onwards, he never laid a finger on me again.

"The bullying at school carried on, but I decided to focus on my studies and set a target for myself to achieve the best GCSE results in the school for that year and I did! I came out with straight As.

"My result was so good that I was offered the Federal Government Scholarship to any university of my choice. That's my story in brief.

"The moral of the story is this: the circumstances of your life may not necessarily lay out before you like a bed of roses. But you can make the decision to lay your own bed yourself, the way you want it. You can succeed if you choose to succeed. That is, irrespective of your background, gender, size, height, shape, ability, or disability, you have the power within you to become whatever you want to be. Almighty God created you with the power to dominate your world. That power is within. With it, you can achieve your dream. That power is the power of choice.

"Make a choice today that you'll focus only on where you want to go, on the person that you want to be. Then write it down on paper, and read it out to yourself daily. You may not see the 'how' to get there now but don't worry, you'll definitely get there.

"Remember: 'Whatever the mind of man can conceive and believe, it can achieve' – said by Napoleon Hill in his book *Think and Grow Rich."*

Then, taking a deep breath and wiping a tear from her eye, she ended her speech with these words: "You, you, and you can definitely become who you want to become because this is planet Earth, and anything is possible! Thank you."

Everyone in the room rose as she stepped off the podium. There was hardly a dry eye in the room. That was by far the most emotional, motivational end-of-year assembly speech that had ever been delivered at St George's High School since I'd joined.

In his closing remarks, the head teacher said it was the best since the school's inception. Then he concluded by specially inviting every member of the school to the fundraising event scheduled for the weekend just to support Mrs. A. H., who had kindly offered to be the teacher in charge of the event. At that last statement, I heaved a sigh of relief. *At last! Our plan for Saturday night stands, thank God!*

Chapter 14

All's Well that Ends Well

I woke up at exactly three that Saturday morning, and as hard as I tried, I couldn't get back to sleep. I was too excited. I wondered if I would be as excited as this on my own wedding day. Well, if you successfully put together a plan to match your teacher with the love of her life, then you would have adrenalin pumping at the same rate as mine that morning. Although we still had several hours before Mrs. A. H. met Mr Lucas Dawson, our plan had so much success written all over it that my mind was completely void of any doubt or fear.

Ethan and I arrived at the school hall at about 4.30 p.m., well more than two hours before the event was to begin. About 6 p.m., the hall was filled to capacity, and Lucas, who'd arrived an hour earlier, was hidden away in the little control room at the top of the hall.

When Mrs. A. H. drove into school that evening at about 6:40pm, she was surprised to find the car park filled. She later explained that she didn't think too much of it but was rather pleased with the turnout and hoped the organizers would raise as much money as possible to support their cause.

As she approached the entrance of the hall, the head teacher stepped out to meet her.

"Catherine, there you are! Oh my days, you look absolutely smashing, Miss!"

"Thank you very much. You look great too!" Taking a look at her watch, she said, "This event has definitely received great publicity; the car park is nearly full!"

"Yes, you're right. The organizers have done a great job!"

"But come to think of it, I didn't believe you'd be here. I thought—"

Interrupting, Mr Oakley explained, "Yeah, you're right, I didn't plan to attend because I had something else planned for the evening, but as it turned out, I got my dates mixed up. The other event is next weekend, so I decided to come and support you, and a few other members of staff and handful of students are here as well. Everyone's in the hall. And pardon my manners, Miss – happy birthday to you, my dear!"

"Ha-ha, that's OK, sir, and thank you very much for the card and flowers. I love them."

"You're most welcome."

"OK, shall we go in? It's nearly seven o'clock."

"Really, how time flies. This way please." He gestured her towards the entrance of the hall.

As soon as she stepped into the hall, the lights went off, and the music went dead.

"What!" she exclaimed, and before she could say another word, the lights suddenly came on as everyone began to sing "Happy Birthday to You."

She couldn't believe her eyes. For a couple of minutes she

stood there completely speechless. She made to turn round and run, but Mr Oakley stood in her way.

He said, "Yes, this is all for you, and you deserve it. Don't you move an inch, because you are the star of tonight's show!"

Everyone began to cheer and clap as Mr Oakley led her to the podium. As she made an attempt to speak, her voice quaked, and she began to sob uncontrollably. Everyone stood up, clapping and cheering.

Amidst all of this clapping and cheering, Lucas began to walk downwards from the top of the hall. At first she couldn't recognize him or work out what was happening, but as she noticed the students walking down with him, she nearly passed out. One could see her hands visibly shaking as she put them over her mouth in utter shock.

When Lucas got to where she stood, he went down on one knee and pulled a ring from his back pocket. Everyone went ballistic because we had carefully hidden this aspect of the plan from everyone, including Mr Oakley.

It was such an emotionally beautiful occasion, and he cleared his throat and asked, "My very dear Catherine, will you marry me?"

The students began to shout "Yes! Yes! Yes!," making kissing sounds.

For the first time ever, Mrs. A. H. looked shy. Then she replied, "Oh, yes Lucas, I will!"

As everyone shouted and clapped, he stood up and gave her a massive bear hug and kissed her.

The head teacher loudly said, "Hmm ... all's well that ends well!"

THE END

ABOUT THE AUTHOR

Gladys Adeleye has in these 20 years, perfected the art of infusing her lessons with funny stories which make her students look forward to every lesson. Her teaching style is so unique that each learner finds concepts easy to understand and recall when required. In their words, she brings Science and Math concepts alive. Her contagious passion and enthusiasm for teaching, make it easy for students to learn and make tangible progress in her classroom.

Printed in Great
Britain
by Amazon